American edition published in 2012 by Andersen Press USA, an imprint of Andersen Press Ltd.
www.andersenpressusa.com

First published in Great Britain in 2012 by Andersen Press Ltd.,
20 Vauxhall Bridge Road, London SW1V 2SA.
Published in Australia by Random House Australia Pty.,
Level 3, 100 Pacific Highway, North Sydney, NSW 2060.

Color separated in Switzerland by Photolitho AG, Zürich.
Printed and bound in Singapore by Tien Wah Press.
Tony Ross has used pen, ink and watercolor in this book.

Library of Congress Cataloging-in-Publication Data Available.
ISBN: 978-0-7613-8993-4
1 – TWP – 12/31/11

A Little Princess Story

I Want to Win!

Tony Ross

Andersen Press USA

The Little Princess liked to win.

At the castle sports day, she entered the running race.

But after just a few strides, she was out of breath.

"Stop!" she commanded the other runners.

"The race must be run in the opposite direction!"

Then she turned around and sprinted back to the start line.
"I win!" she cried.

"I want to win!" she said when she played games at home,
and since everyone lost on purpose, she usually did.

But at school it was different.
There were trophies there for everything . . .

. . . and the Little Princess wanted to win them all!

She tried her HARDEST at math,

but her cousin won the Math Trophy.

She tried her HARDEST at painting,

but Polly won the Painting Trophy.

She tried her HARDEST at writing her poem,

but Poppy won the Poetry Trophy.

She tried her HARDEST at science,

but Darren won the Science Trophy.

"It's not fair!" sobbed the Little Princess. "I've tried my very hardest, but I haven't won anything!"

When all the big trophies had been taken from the shelf . . .

. . . there was just one little one left that nobody had noticed.

But it turned out to be the best trophy of all, because it was for . . .

. . . TRYING THE HARDEST, and because she *had* tried
so hard, the Little Princess won it fair and square!

Other Little Princess Books

I Want a Party!

I Want My Light On!

I Want to Do It Myself!

I Want Two Birthdays!